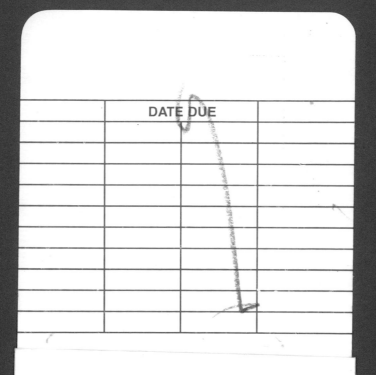

VERNA AARDEMA

KOI AND THE KOLA NUTS

A TALE FROM LIBERIA

illustrated by JOE CEPEDA

AN ANNE SCHWARTZ BOOK

ATHENEUM BOOKS for YOUNG READERS

To my sister-in-law, Kay Norberg
—V. A.

To my mother, *con amor*
—J. C.

Koi and the Kola Nuts is a revision of a story that was included in Verna Aardema's book, *Tales from the Story Hat,* published by Coward, McCann, and Geoghegan, Inc., New York, 1960. That book is out of print and the rights have been returned to Mrs. Aardema.

The original source is the story "Koi and His Heritage," in a booklet entitled *Nemo and Other Stories,* published by the National Fundamental Education Centre, Klay, Liberia, 1954, no copyright. That booklet was used in the "Each One Teach One" campaign to teach adults to read, and as a textbook in mission schools.

❋

Atheneum Books for Young Readers An imprint of Simon & Schuster Children's Publishing Division 1230 Avenue of the Americas New York, New York 10020 Text copyright © 1999 by Verna Aardema Illustrations copyright © 1999 by Joe Cepeda
Book design by Michael Nelson The text of this book is set in Cafeteria. The illustrations are rendered in oil paint. Printed in Hong Kong
10   9   8   7   6   5   4
Library of Congress Cataloging-in-Publication Data Aardema, Verna. Koi and the kola nuts : a tale from Liberia / retold by Verna Aardema ; illustrated by Joe Cepeda.–1st ed. p. cm. "An Anne Schwartz book." Summary: An African folktale in which the son of the chief must make his way in the world with only a sackful of kola nuts and the help of some creatures that he has treated with kindness. ISBN 0-689-81760-6 [1. Folklore–Liberia.] I. Cepeda, Joe, ill. II. Title. PZ8.1.A213Ko 1999 398.2'096662'02–dc21 [E] 97-46713

GLOSSARY

Chief Fulikolli (Foo-lih-KOH-lee)

Chief Ogumefu (Oh-goo-MAY-foo)

Forest Devil: An entertainer and storyteller who wore an ugly mask and several overlapping grass skirts as a costume.

Kinja (KEEN-ja): A carrying frame made of sticks lashed together, worn upon the back, and held in place by straps about the shoulders and across the forehead.

Koi (KOY): The Liberian name of the hero in the source story, "Koi and His Heritage," from *Nemo and Other Stories*.

Kola nuts (KOH-la nuts): Kola nuts grow wild in West Africa. Each seed pod contains several red and white nuts which are shaped like horse chestnuts. They are chewed for their flavor, as well as for a stimulant or medication. They are also used in making kola-flavored drinks.

Liberia (Li-BEER-e-a): A small country on the west coast of Africa which was settled by freed American slaves.

Medicine Ring: An important ring containing a signet design which could be pressed into a spot of melted wax to authenticate a document.

Rainmaker: A tribesman whose function was to pray for rain. He offered libations by pouring palm beer on the ground.

Note: The ideophones—words that mimic actual sounds—that appear throughout are spelled phonetically.

One day in a village in Liberia, the headman, Chief Ogumefu, died. After the funeral ceremonies, an old Wise Man came to divide the royal possessions. To each of the three oldest sons, he counted out so many sheep, so many cows, and so many tusks of ivory.

But Koi, the youngest, was still on his way home from hunting–so he got nothing. He arrived only in time to see his brothers hurrying off with their animals and ivory.

"Old man," he said, "where is my share?"

The old Wise Man said, "You are too late. I can't undo what is done." He looked about, and when his eyes fell on a scraggly little kola tree, he gave that to Koi.

"Why are you cheating me?" cried Koi. "I, too, am a son of the chief!"

The Wise Man stared at Koi for a long moment—but his mouth stood still.

Then he shuffled off, his sandals scuffing, *ras, ras, ras,* upon the path.

Koi sat down to ponder his plight. But soon he jumped up, saying, "What sitting won't solve, travel will! There's a whole world out there, and I'm going to explore it!" He picked the kola nuts from his tree, wrapped them in a mat, tied the mat on a *kinja,* and swung the load onto his back.

Koi set out on a path that led north from the village. He had not gone far when he met a little snake slithering, *wasa-wusu, wasa-wusu,* down the path. Now and then it would stop and gaze up into the trees.

Koi asked, "What are you looking for, my friend?"

"A kola tree," said the snake. "My mother is ill, and she needs kola medicine."

Koi said, "I can give you a kola nut." And he reached back into his kinja and pulled one right out.

"Thank you," said the snake. "I hope I can help you someday." And it wriggled away.

Koi went on and on. Before long he met an army of ants, marching four abreast in an endless column. The ant leader called in a tiny voice, "Mister, do you know where we can find a kola tree? We ate the nuts in the Forest Devil's basket, and if we don't replace them, *quick, quick, quick,* he will squash us all!"

"How many do you need, little one?" asked Koi.

"As many as all his fingers and all his toes." The ant counted its own feet, and said, "Six."

"But the Forest Devil isn't an ant," Koi said. "He's a man!" He gave the ants ten nuts for his fingers and ten for his toes.

"Thank you," they cried, and they trudged off with their heavy load, panting, *uh, uh, uh.*

After many days, Koi came to a mountain with a path zigzagging up its steep slope. "Yo," he groaned. "I don't want to climb that. But if I don't, I'll never know what's on the other side." To gain strength, he lay down under a tree to nap.

Presently Koi was awakened by sobbing, *Waaah, waaah, waaah!* He looked around and saw a crusty old crocodile collapsed near the path, his tears making small puddles in the sand.

"Oh, poor Crocodile!" cried Koi. "What terrible trouble has caught you?"

"I ate the Rainmaker's dog," the crocodile replied. "Now he's going to zap me with a lightning bolt if I don't repay him before sundown." Then he added sadly, "If I had known whose dog it was, I would have eaten someone else's."

"What is the Rainmaker's price?" Koi asked.

"A big bag of kola nuts."

"Dry your eyes, Crocodile," said Koi. "Look. Here are enough nuts to pay for *two* dogs!" He unfolded a corner of his mat to show what was inside. "I'm giving them to you." Then he strapped the kinja onto the broad back of the crocodile.

"Thank you," said the crocodile with a toothy smile. Then he trundled off, his great tail lashing, *belong-belang, belong-belang.*

Happy to be relieved of his burden, Koi jauntily climbed up and over the mountain. Farther on he came to a village.

A guard at the gate stopped him. "Who enters the domain of Chief Fulikolli?" he asked.

Koi was still wearing his shabby hunting garb and was covered with dust from the trail. Still, he stood tall and said, "I am Koi, a son of the great Chief Ogumefu."

The guard studied him. "Hmm, you talk big for a beggar," he said, but he went to fetch the chief.

"I suppose you are here to try to win my beautiful daughter and half my chiefdom," Chief Fulikolli said gruffly, for suitors had been coming from far and near.

Koi raised his eyebrows in surprise. He felt as though a ripe plum had fallen into his basket! "Indeed I have," he answered.

"To obtain that prize, you will have to *earn* it," said the chief.

"First you must chop down that palm tree so that it falls toward the forest."
And he pointed to a tree that leaned sharply toward the village.

Koi shuddered when he saw it. But all he said was, "I will try."

So an ax was given to Koi, and he was left alone.

Soon Koi heard a familiar sound—*wasa-wusu, wasa-wusu.* There, coming toward
him, was the snake whom he had helped.

"I've tracked you a long way," the snake said. "The kola nut cured my mother,
and she sends her thanks."

"How kind of you to come and tell me," Koi said. "But now I have a problem.
See that palm tree? I must chop it down so that it falls toward the forest."

"That's not possible!" exclaimed the snake. "It leans the wrong way."

"I know," said Koi.

"I'll get my uncles, the pythons," the snake said. "Maybe they can help."

At moonrise, the snake returned with three pythons. The huge snakes wrapped their necks around the palm and their tails around a nearby mango tree. They held the palm firmly while Koi chopped, *pim-pen, pim-pen, pim-pen*. When the last palm fiber snapped, the pythons lifted the tree and dropped it, *ka-boom*, toward the forest.

The next morning Chief Fulikolli saw the fallen palm tree with Koi standing proudly beside it. "Young man," he said, "you have done well . . . so far. But we have another challenge for you. We have scattered a big basket of rice over a field, and you must pick up every grain in the dark of night."

That night Koi took a basket to the field. As he was sifting handfuls of soil, feeling for rice, an ant crawled into his palm.

"Mister," it said, "aren't you the one who gave us kola nuts when we needed them?"

"Probably," said Koi.

"Those kola nuts saved us from the Forest Devil!" said the ant.

"Good!" said Koi. "Now maybe you can help me. I have to pick up all this rice before morning."

"My people will do it," said the ant. And soon the ground was crawling with ants, all picking up rice. *Tik, tik, tik,* the hard little grains rained into the basket. Before long, the field was clean.

In the morning Chief Fulikolli found Koi with a full basket of rice waiting quietly beside his door. "You have succeeded again," he said. "But there is one more task—the most difficult of all. And if you fail, you will forfeit your life. I shall throw my Medicine Ring into the river, and you must retrieve it before another day dawns."

Before Koi could answer, the chief took off his big brass ring and hurled it, *kwa-cha*, far out into the water.

As the chief was leaving, Koi called after him, "I can't even swim!" Then he sat down alone to watch the swiftly flowing river as it gurgled, *pon, pon, pon, sah,* over the rocks. And it seemed to be saying, "This is the end. This is the end. This is the end. . . ."

It wasn't long before night came on. Stars appeared, one by one at first, and soon the sky was spangled with them. In this dim eerie starlight Koi discerned the long body of a crocodile streaking toward him.

The crocodile grinned at Koi and said, "Remember me?"

"Oh, yes," said Koi. "But now I need your help. The chief of this land threw his Medicine Ring into the river, and I have to retrieve it by sunup, or I shall be killed."

The crocodile said, "You saved my life. Now it's my turn to save yours."
All night the great beast worked, raking the river bottom, surfacing
only to breathe. As the sun peeped above the horizon, he came up
waving the ring on one of his claws.

That morning Chief Fulikolli emerged from his hut to find Koi waiting for him with the Medicine Ring. The chief slipped the ring on his finger. "Koi, you have performed all of the tasks," he said. "You have won my daughter and half my chiefdom. I now name you Chief Koi." Then he called, "Fula, come and meet the man you are going to marry."

At once, out from her royal hut there stepped the most beautiful girl Koi had ever seen. She ran to him with outstretched arms. For she had been watching from her doorway and had fallen in love with him as he risked his life to win her.

It was a grand wedding. During the feasting Chief Koi said to himself, "Now I know it to be true: Do good and good will come back to you—in full measure and overflowing."